T0374083

Cherry Mouse Babies: Let's Draw!

AuthorHouse™ UK
1663 Liberty Drive
Bloomington, IN 47403 USA
www.authorhouse.co.uk
Phone: 0800.197.4150

Published by AuthorHouse 06/04/2018

ISBN: 978-1-5462-8879-4 (sc)
ISBN: 978-1-5462-8878-7 (e)

Library of Congress Control Number: 2018906555

Print information available on the last page.

This book is printed on acid-free paper.

authorHOUSE®

Cherry Mouse Babies Characters:

Let's Draw!

Painter's Name:______________________________

Painter's Age:______________________________

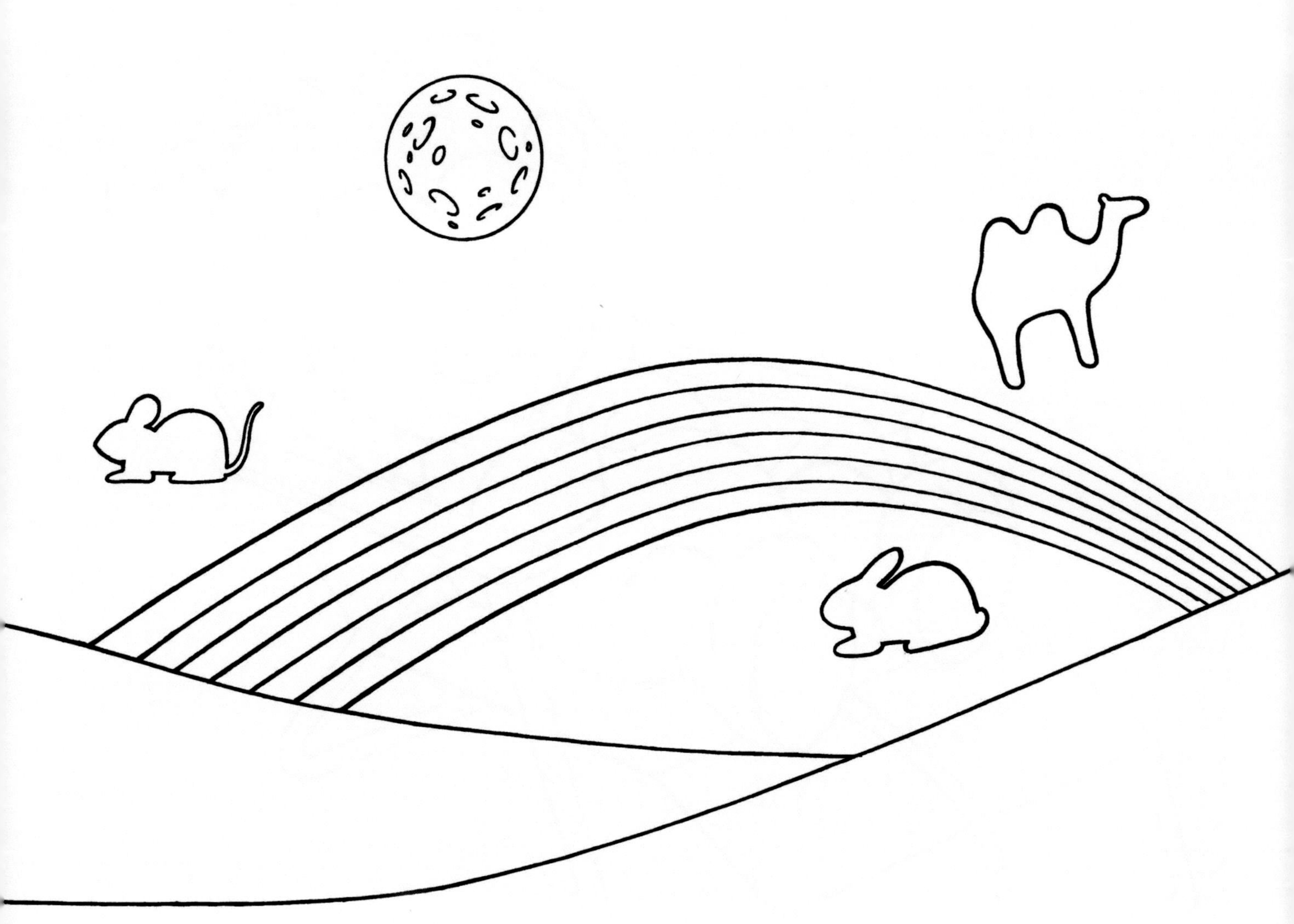

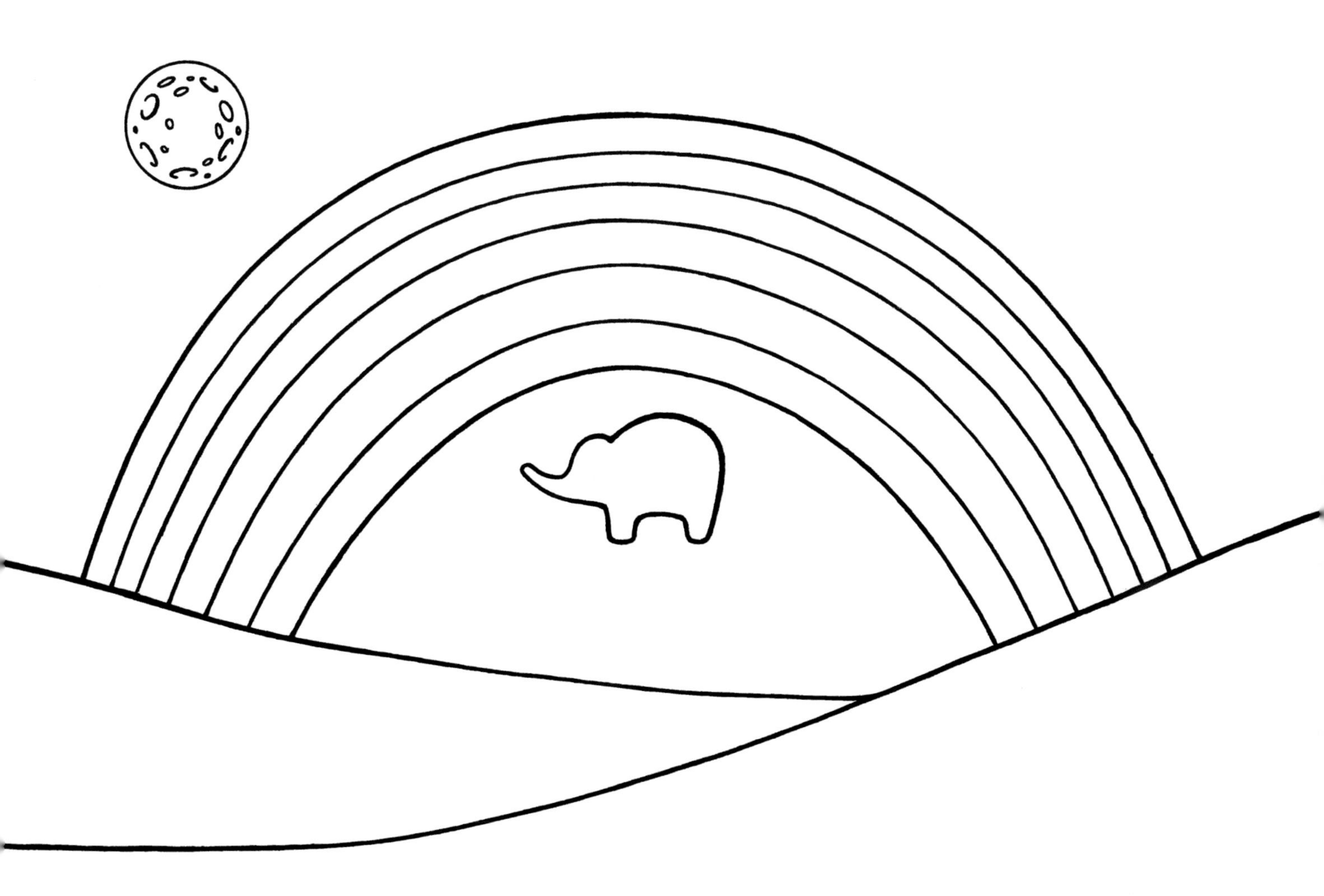

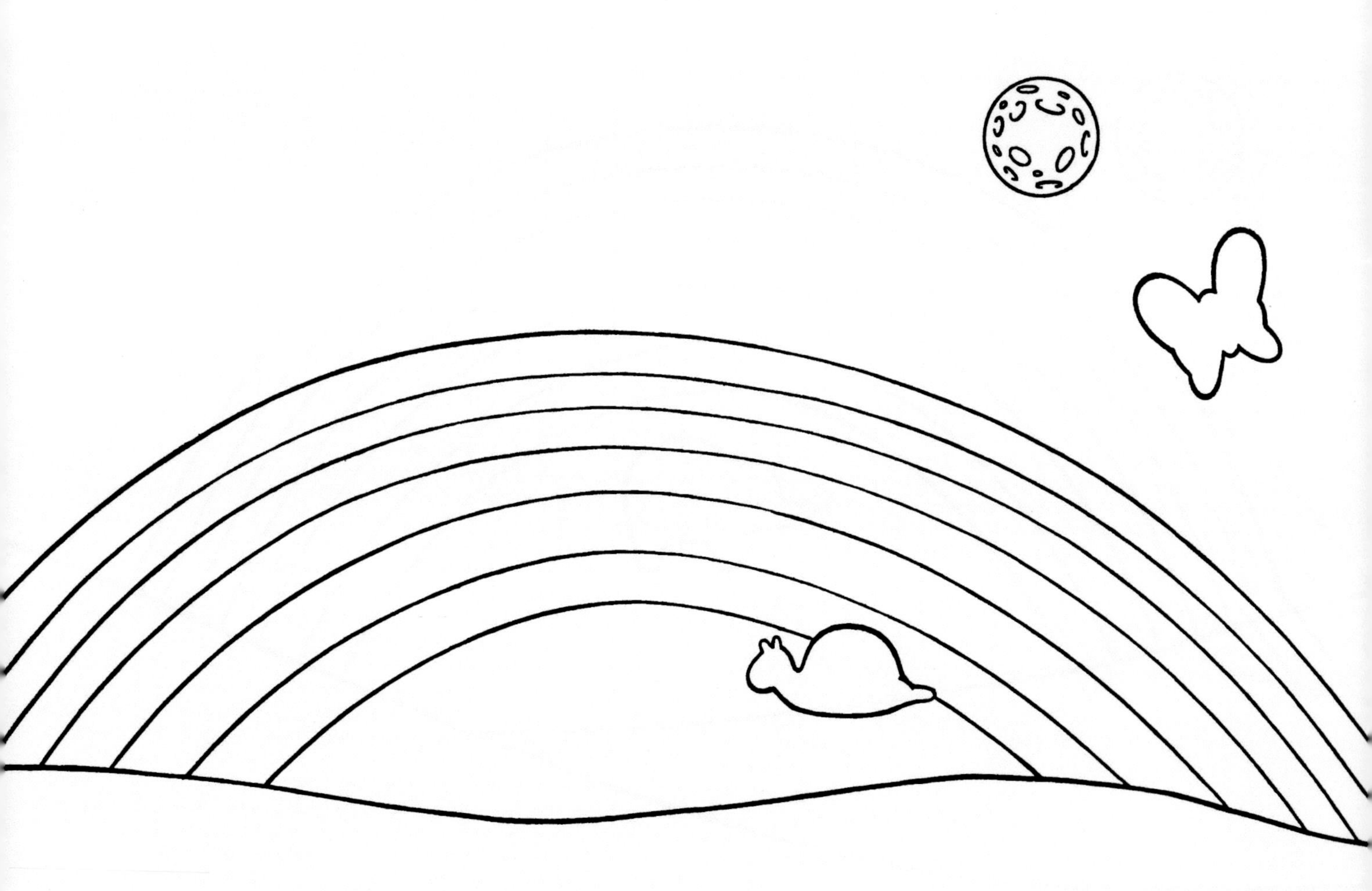

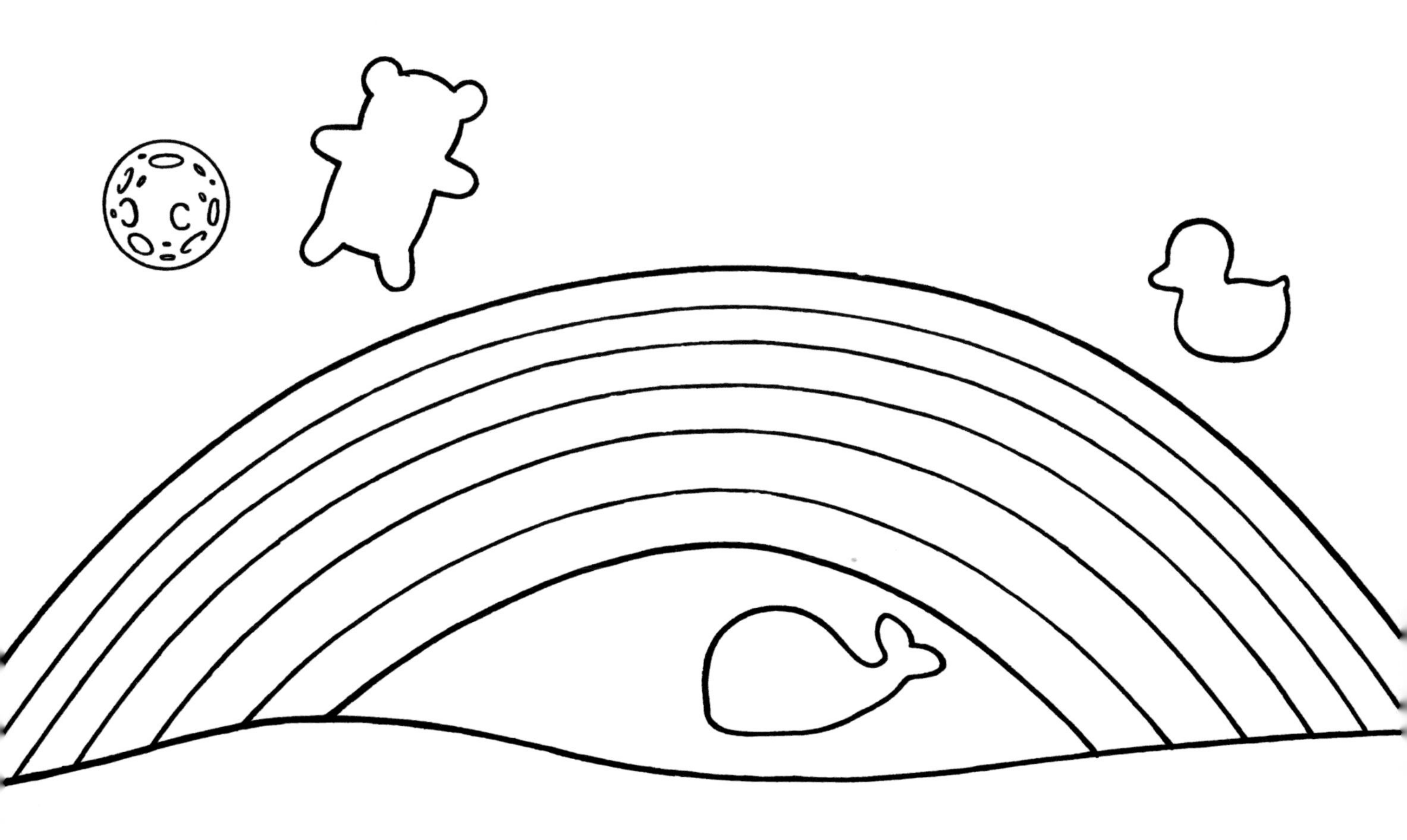

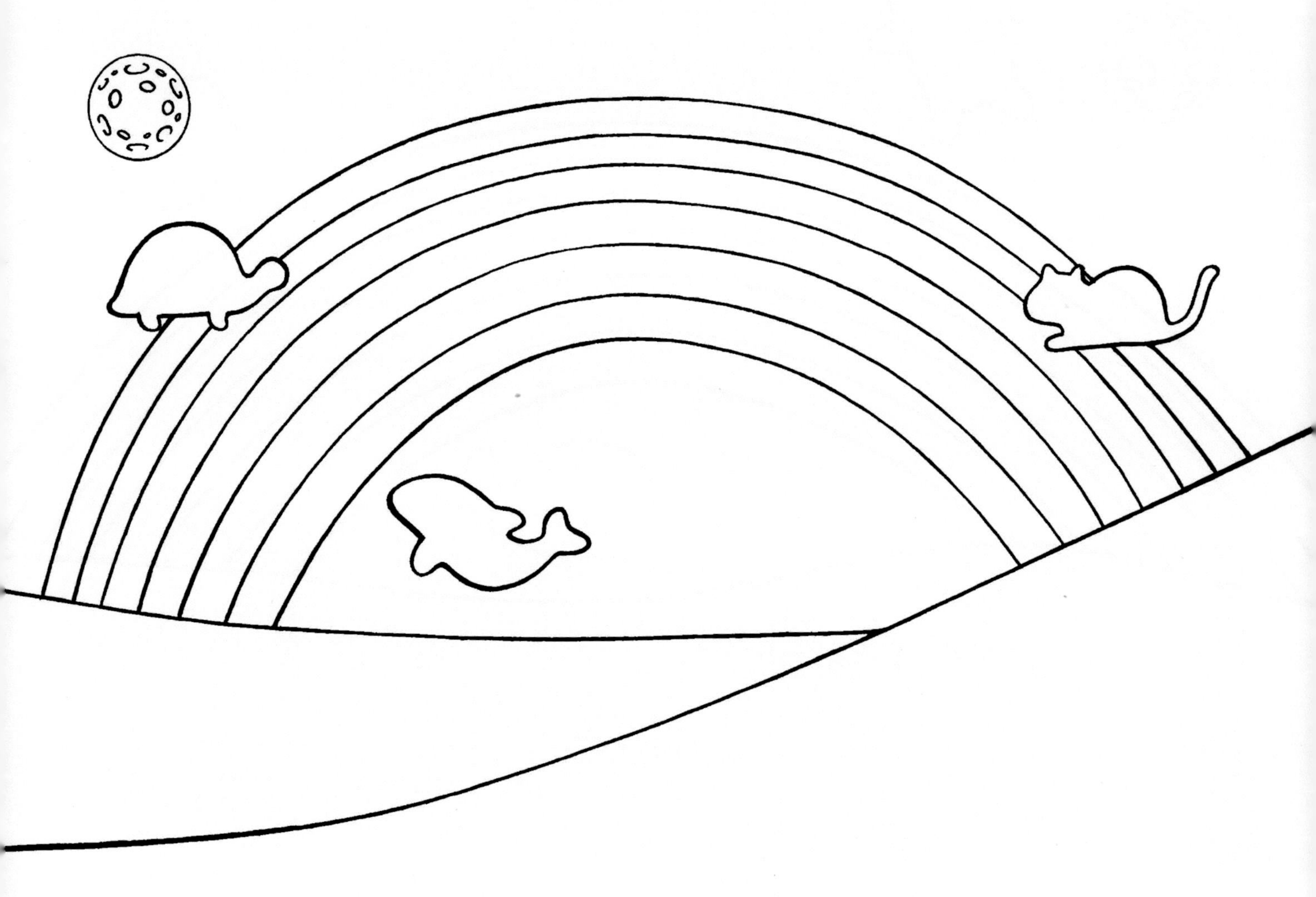

A Cherry Mouse Babies Story:
Let's Draw!

Painter's Name:______________________________

Painter's Age:______________________________

Printed in the United States
By Bookmasters